Monster
in the
Wall

by: Blanch A. Nutting

To order additional copies of this book, contact:
Xlibris Corporation
1-888-795-4274
www.Xlibris.com
Orders@Xlibris.com

One Saturday when my Mom had to go away, my brother Brandon and I went to spend the afternoon at Nana and Papa's. We liked going there, because there were so many things to do.

Behind our grandparents' house was a huge hill with lots of trees, a brook and many trails. Nana often took us hiking on those trails.

There were also four ponds to play around.

Besides the outside fun spots, we could play with Sir William, the furry dog, and Phoebe, the long-haired cat.

Brandon and I played outside hiking and exploring with Nana. If we went too far away, Nana yelled out, "Wait for me, guys."

She always took my hand while crossing the gurgling brook saying, "Step here, honey, on this big rock." Nana often called us 'honey'. I guess because she loved us. After our trek up the hill and down again, we returned home.

While Nana prepared supper for Papa and us,
we ran into the living room to play with the animals.

When Phoebe spied us, she took off;
so, we raced after her down to the cellar.

Phoebe was scared of us for some reason; so, after a few minutes, she disappeared. Brandon and I searched every nook and cranny in Nana's messy cellar, but we couldn't find her. We figured she had run upstairs to the safety of Nana's arms.

Brandon and I kept playing for awhile looking at old things stored in the cellar, when Brandon spotted a hole in the wall behind the furnace.

He went to check it out, then peeked into the hole. With a scream, he ran back to me yelling, "There's a monster with big, bulgy eyes in there, Gavin!"

I was scared but wanted to see for myself just what he was talking about, so I crept over to the hole and peered in. Sure enough huge, blue eyeballs stared out from the blackness.

"Help! Help! Nana!" we yelled as we dashed up the stairs.

"Boys, what's going on?" she asked. "There's a monster in the wall!" we screamed.

"What?" "There's a monster in the wall!" we repeated. Nana looked kind of strange, so we added, "Come, quick and see!" We all rushed downstairs to the clean-out hole for the fireplace. "Look in there, Nana," we yelled, pointing.

Nana bent over and peered in. She soon chuckled and reached into the dark hole drawing out a dirty, white cat.

"Phoebe," Brandon and I shouted together. "How did you get in there?" After admitting to Nana that we had chased Phoebe, Nana sat us down to discuss our fear while she cleaned Phoebe's coat and paws.

"You know people fear things they don't know much about like you boys did with the huge eyes in the black hole. Even grown-ups fear things they don't understand. Now that you know it was Phoebe in the clean-out hole, you aren't afraid of what you saw. Right?"

"Right," we agreed.

"In the future, when you are startled by something, remember there is usually an explanation for the fright. Try to calm down and recall what happened today.
You just might be able to laugh at your fear of other so-called 'monsters' you meet in life as we are doing right now."

The End

CPSIA information can be obtained
at www.ICGtesting.com
Printed in the USA
LVIC080933070413
327703LV00002BB

9 781465 387172